PELEE ISLAND STORIES

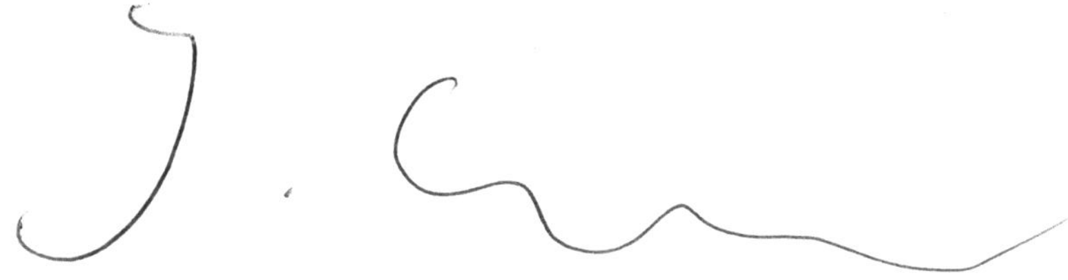

TANYA COOVADIA

PELEE ISLAND STORIES

CRABAPPLE MEWS COLLECTIVE

Crabapple Mews Collective
Calgary, Alberta
www.crabapplemewscollective.com

ISBN 978-0-9920795-6-7

Editing by Jane Cawthorne, E.D. Morin, Lou Morin and Inge Bremer-Trueman
Book design by Natalie Olsen, Kisscut Design
Author photo by Adam Coovadia

Printed in Canada by BookPOD University of Toronto Bookstore

I would like to dedicate this tiny collection to the person who has occupied the largest space in my life: my best friend and life partner Adam Coovadia. For the last twenty years he has supported my work in every way possible. My successes are his.

CONTENTS

I AM CANDI

I AM CANDI

She fights the pain but she's losing. Her legs straighten and contract, knees draw toward her taut belly, then unbend. Her toes point toward the foot of the scuttled bed. She stifles her cries with both hands, rolls and writhes to the huff of her own, clutched-in breath. Her eyes stretch round with fear.

Slow minutes pass as the pain relaxes its grip. She rises from the bed and puts both feet on the floor with care, wipes her forehead with the back of her arm, and pushes herself with both hands off the bed. Her hair, the colour and heft of half-dried hay, scatters itself around her pink face, settles down her fallen shoulders, and sticks to the back of her sodden neck.

A faded yellow dress, enlivened by a pattern of small pink flowers, hugs her at an uncomfortable angle. She tugs at its waist and moves slowly, listing to the left in a dignified asymmetry. Her face tightens around uncertain eyes.

Her smudged cordless phone is just within reach on a plastic lawn chair that acts as a side table. Through the dim light, she navigates the debris humped around the room, trails along the hallway and down the staircase. As the pain banks, she plots a course around piles of clothing, magazines and trash, steps over heaps of old linens and two cases of Diet Coke to reach the kitchen. She peels a magnet from the refrigerator. Large, red letters say, "(800) TREAT-ME," and smaller, blue numbers say, "(800) 873-2865."

She squeezes through the bathroom door and closes it behind her.

With her weight against the sink, she holds the phone in one hand and squints at the fridge magnet in the other.

She glances back and forth between them, back and forth, back and forth, sucks in her lower lip, and presses the phone's buttons, one by one. She puts the phone to her ear and waits.

She listens for a moment, then nods her head. "My name is Candi," she says in a voice low with urgency. "I'm goin' on thirty and I live on Pelee Island. My tummy is hurtin' real bad. Real bad."

"I am *goin'* on thirty," she repeats, frowning. "I'm a be thirty in July."

She listens, nods. "Well, it's better right now," she says, frowning, "but it keeps comin' back, eh?"

This time, as she listens, she throws up a hand, a backhanded swat at frustration, and says, "No!" in a hiss. "There's no hospital on Pelee!" she says. "That's why I'm callin' *you*."

This time, as she listens, her face reddens.

"Yes, we got René – she's the nurse but I don't want to call her because Uncle Ed might be mad! I never should've told nobody, except it hurts like hell."

She drops her rusted panties to the floor, kicks them to the side, and sits on the toilet. She waits.

"I'm on the toilet right now, but nothin's comin' out," she says.

She frowns.

"I told you I *can't* call the nurse. Uncle Ed's comin' back from the mainland tomorrow! He's goin' to be pissed *off!*"

"Oh boy, here we go again!" She expels a quick gasp.

She wraps her arms under her belly. Her forehead creases and the splotches of pink on her cheeks deepen. She casts a glance toward the closed door and pulls her voice to a grunt.

"A while ago. . . I made a number two. . . and I went number one. A *lot* of number one. . . but nothin's comin' now."

"Nope, I didn't eat nothin' funny," she says. "Just a fried baloney samdich and a Diet Coke."

She holds the phone away from her ear, looks at it, and shakes her head. She speaks into it as though it were a microphone, keeping her ears free of its chatter.

"Yep, it tasted okay," she says, firm in this conviction. "Nope, I don't have a headache! What are you, some kind a retard?"

Even as she utters this word, she winces. Her mouth closes, and she shakes her head and sighs. She puts the phone back to her ear.

"I'm sorry," she says. "I never should've said that. It's just that my tummy still hurts, and I'm scared 'cause it's getting worser—wait, what's that now?"

She listens, shaking her head.

"No, dummy," she says with a snort. "Uncle Ed is my stepdad."

"No, I don't got no boyfriend," she says, and her face curves to hint at a smile. "But the guys *do* think I'm really popular, eh? They always take me out to parties a lot. I'm the only girl, and I get them beers, too, because I'm old enough. That makes them think I'm even more popular."

When Candi was little, she was the only girl in third grade at the island school, and she wasn't popular. Sometimes, the other kids would tease and push her. Other times, they ignored her, not speaking back to her when she talked to them. Sometimes they just walked away. Except Rocky. He once showed her a dead raccoon under a tree at the edge of the playground. "Cool, eh?" he asked, and she agreed.

She's thinking about Rocky and smiling in her incomplete way when a new, sharper pain catches her by surprise. She doubles over, the toilet seat squeaking, her face clenched around a silenced scream. She begins to pant.

"Look, lady, can't you do something?" she says to the phone, her voice a series of grunts. "My tummy's gettin' worser again."

She drops the phone and squirms around her straining belly. Bursts of damp stain her mouldering dress. Tears splash from her eyes, spread across her burning cheeks. She writhes. Her body seeks a position that will pull the cramp smooth.

She moans into her hands and wishes it were still yesterday.

Yesterday, the guys were supposed to come. Ryan had given her a ride home from the store. He said maybe he would be by to pick her up later. Yesterday, when he said that, her tummy gave a little lurch of joy.

She watched him pull out, tires spinning up the gravel of Ruggles Road, driving off so fast in his newly-washed, so-shiny red Ford pickup. Then she hurried to put her bread and baloney and Diet Coke in the fridge, and went back to the front door to scan the road north to south and back again. She stood there in the doorway until her legs became numb, but the guys weren't back yet. She went inside to wait, leaving the door ajar. She brushed her teeth again, because Uncle Ed always said there's nothing worse than stinky breath on a girl. Nothing. Then she heard a truck coming from far off, and hurried back to the door. It still wasn't the guys, though. Just Charlie Bray driving by in his rusty blue Dodge, clouds of fishing net billowing up in the truck bed. Charlie held up a hand and nodded, and she nodded and waved back as his truck faded into the dust.

She went back to the living room, dug the remote from under the stuff on the couch, lay down and turned on the TV, but none of her shows were on. Her dress was squeezing her middle, and she squirmed and rearranged its tight folds until it clung to her armpits, instead of her belly. She gave up, and pushed off the couch to find something more comfortable.

All of her dresses were too small, now. It reminded her of when *she* was small, back when her mother was happy. Her mother used to say all the time that Candi grew like a weed. But Candi wasn't *supposed* to grow nowadays. She knew that.

Still waiting for the guys to pull up, she rummaged through the clothes on the floor of her closet, finally pulling on a faded pink skirt that used to belong to her mom. It was too tight, but not as much, so she left it on, pulling Uncle Ed's greying Molson Canadian t-shirt over top.

It didn't matter, anyway, because the guys never did come, although she waited until the fireflies started blinking, then stopped, until the mosquitoes, taking advantage of the open door, had drunk their fill, until her mom came downstairs to use the bathroom and went back up. Candi waited, blinking herself to sleep while the man on TV got all excited about washing cars with these new improved rags.

The snore bubbling at the back of her throat was cut in half when Uncle Ed, smelling like the tavern, slammed the front door behind him and yelled at her to get the fuck to bed.

When the pain finally subsides, Candi lets her hands slip off her mouth in relief. She pulls a few handfuls of toilet paper off the roll and wipes her eyes, the back of her neck, her bosom. She retrieves the phone from the floor.

"That's better," she tells the phone. "Phew."

"Yeah, I'm still here," she tells it. "The hurtin's goin' away again."

She listens, nodding. "Yeah, maybe you're right. I should call René to have a look. But, Uncle Ed – he don't like that sort of thing. Showin' yourself to people. It's dirty."

"What? No, a course not! I *never* shown myself to the guys." The corners of her mouth are coy. "They only want to party in the dark anyways," she says. "That's what they say. They only want to see me in the dark. That's a joke, eh? Ha! Because in the dark, you *can't* see."

A new lady is talking to her on the phone, now, but Candi isn't listening.

"Another joke they say is that they wanna piece of Candi. 'Who wants a piece of Candi? Come get your Candi right here!' Ha! It's funny, eh? 'Cause I'm something you get to eat up. Like a treat! Ha ha!"

Candi notices the lady is still talking, and this time she listens. "Wait, what?"

"Yeah, there's a mirror in here," she says. "It's sittin' on the sink."

Her smile snaps shut. She shakes her head. "I'm sorry, you want me to look at my what, now?" she says.

"My *what*?" she says, half rising from the toilet, "Are you kidding me! No, I'm not gonna do that! That is so inappropriat-ed! Where's the other lady? Can't I talk to her again? Please!"

She sits back down, propelled by a whoosh of breath. "Oh no," she says. "It's hurtin' again."

She expels the creaky moan she lacks the energy to suppress, puts down the phone, and prepares to ride out the pain. She tries to think a comforting thought, but instead thinks of a morning, the one after the last night the guys *had* come, and moans again.

That morning none of her shows were on, so she went for a walk to pick the blackberries that grew dusty alongside the gravel of Ruggles Road. Standing amongst the thorny canes, she picked and ate, staining her hands with the deep purple of the juice, reminding herself not to wipe them on her dress. The thump of a heavy boot made her jump in her shoes. Too late, she tried to hide in stillness. But she'd never been that still.

"Candi! Candi, goddammit, where the hell are you!"

Uncle Ed always knew where she was. And he was always mad.

"You know you're supposed to be in your bed after ten," he said, grabbing her upper arm, his fingers making points of pain that she would remember the next day. "What in hell were you up to last night, you goddamn slut?"

"Nothing," Candi said. Usually, she didn't talk, but this time she did.

"Better be nothing! Better keep to your fucking self, you know what's good for you."

"Okay," said Candi.

"What? What'd you say to me?"

"Okay."

"You bet your fat ass it's okay! You already cause enough trouble, without you running all over hell and high water!"

Then Uncle Ed moved off. He had another field to harvest and didn't have time for her crap. With her mother sleeping all night and day and Candi as useful as tits on a bull, he had enough on his hands. She knew that.

This memory is *not* a comfort. It's making the spasms pull harder and, as Candi covers her mouth again with her hands, she tries to think of another.

Sometimes, when René goes to people's houses to make them better, Candi gets to go too. That's her second favourite thing, because René is her favourite person, even though she loves her mother and even though the guys are the most fun. When Candi helps René, though, it's an important thing to do. Last winter Jim Harper broke his arm and Candi had to hold him still just right, and René pulled and pulled at his poor arm, and then wrapped it in wet strips that hardened into a broken arm cast. Jim had cried and yelled then, but now his arm is just fine. And Candi had helped it be.

Now *she's* the one making noises like Jim made when his arm was all bent. But the pain is getting softer. It's almost gone. She picks up the phone.

"I'm back," she tells it, then sits up straight, her head cocked, as a shuffling sound stops outside the bathroom door.

"Wait," she whispers to the phone. "My mom's up. Be quiet."

"Candi? You in there?" Her mom's voice is scratchy, but sweet.

"Mom? You okay?" Candi says.

"I'm okay, baby, I'm just tired," her mom says, opening the bathroom door. "You okay?"

"No, I'm not so good. I got a tummy ache, real bad."

Candi's mom sighs and leans against the doorway as if she's rolling over in an upright bed.

"You okay?" she asks again, hoping for another answer, and this time, Candi gives it.

"Yeah, I'm okay."

"You going to be in there long, honey? I gotta use the can."

Candi tries to keep a wince inside, but it creeps out anyway. She gasps, then tells her mom, "Do you gotta do a number one? Can you go outside, maybe?"

Candi's mom nods and turns to go, but she stops.

She looks in Candi's eyes.

"Feel better, okay, Kiddo MacGoo?" she says.

Kiddo MacGoo is a nickname that Candi's mom used to call her. Most of the time, she doesn't call her that any more.

"Yeah, I'm okay. Don't worry."

Still looking in Candi's eyes, her mom turns the tiny knob on the handle, locking the bathroom door. Then she leaves, closing it behind her.

"I love you, baby girl," she says through the closed door. "Good night."

"Okay," Candi says, "I love you, too. Get some sleep, eh?"

Candi listens for a moment. When she hears the clunk of the back door closing, she winces and picks up the phone.

"Hello," she says, "I think you're right. I gotta call René. That one hurt real bad."

She tilts her head with the phone.

"Okay, I'll go lie down just as soon as I get off this toilet, 'cause I still feel like I gotta poop real bad."

She listens for a moment, and sighs.

"Okay! I'm gettin' the mirror. Man alive, you are not appropriat-ed, at, all."

She winces as she reaches over to the vanity and picks up the small red hand mirror she's never before had occasion to use. The phone continues to babble.

"Hold your horses, there, Chief. I'm lookin'!" she says to the impatient voice, thrusts the mirror between her legs, and tilts it toward her eyes.

"Oh my *God!*" she says. "How'd *that* get in there?"

The pain returns in a gust, a throbbing, squeezing assault, and she throws the mirror against the wall reflexively, as though to ward it off. The phone falls from her hand and screams throw themselves out of her, first one, then another. She pants and groans and screams again. Her feet thump up and down on either side of the toilet, stomping the phone. She exhales in a long grunt, her face a dull shade of scarlet. Then she does it again. She spreads out and mutates, sharp here, dull there, pain radiating from so many places that each one dulls the other.

There's a splash. Candi takes a deep breath. "Ow," she says, as she picks up the phone. "That's better. I feel like something got torned, though. Man oh man. That one really hurt."

She glances down as she leans forward for the toilet paper. She drops the phone to the floor.

"Oh my God!" she says. "There's a baby!—there's a baby! In the toilet! I swear to God there's a tiny little baby with its head down in the toilet! Wait, I gotta get it out. I gotta get it *out*!"

The baby is slippery, covered with god-knows-what and it smells funny too, but Candi picks it out of the toilet and holds it to her. She and the baby look at each other, wide-eyed.

The baby takes a deep breath and proceeds to wail. Candi yells at the phone on the floor.

"Hello, lady? That thing up there was a baby! I had a baby!"

She regards the tiny, slimy, smelly thing and her unfinished smile completes itself.

"Awwww. He's cryin'. He's *such* a cute little baby. I just love him to death."

Through the baby's wails, she hears a gentle tread in the hallway—not Uncle Ed, not her mom.

"Candi? Are you in there?" a voice calls.

"Wait," Candi says to the phone on the floor. "You called René! René?" she says. "I'm in here!"

She lifts the hem of her skirt, and wraps it as well as she can around the baby's brand new body. Clutching this noisy, smelly, tiny person to her with one arm, she unlocks the bathroom door. René stands in the doorway, her mouth open with surprise.

"Look René! I got a baby! A boy! A cute, cute, *cute* little baby boy! Isn't he *noisy*?" Candi's face is angular with unfamiliar joy. She lifts her baby so that she can look into his face.

"Hi there," she says. "Hi little baby."

His cries subside, and he regards her with old man eyes.

"He's my baby, right René? I can keep him! He's mine! Oh my God! I can't believe I'm so lucky!" Candi says.

René doesn't respond. Candi doesn't notice.

"I wonder what his name is, eh?"

FALLING IN LOVE

FALLING IN LOVE

If they had chosen to do so, both Rocky and Tammy could have identified the exact moment the act changed from one thing to its opposite. It was equidistant between two words: Rocky's soft "Lizzie" and Tammy's loud "No!"

Rocky's "Lizzie" was involuntary, Tammy knew, his breath pushing warmly into her ear. She almost failed to hear the word, its sibilance hushed in the sensation of his boner bumping between her legs and her shy centre moving awkwardly to meet his.

The second word, "No!" was pushed out of her as his boner wedged itself into her now reluctant opening. "No," she said again, shaking her head as the word "Lizzie" made her make sense of things. "No, no, no, no, no," she said, huffing it out to the rhythm of his thrusts.

He pretended not to hear, the roar of his epiphany drowning out her refusal. He came into her, still thrusting wetly, slowly, through his own semen.

"No!" She pushed him away and jumped from the moss-covered rock which was now the place where she lost her virginity. "Didn't you hear me? I said, 'No!'"

It was too late. Rocky's eyes held a satisfied, enlightened look, as though he was resting after a major accomplishment, as though he had learned something important, something life-changing. In fact, he was picturing the other guys grasping what he had done, who he had become. They would notice a new firmness in his eyes, he was sure. He wouldn't talk about Tammy, of course, but he couldn't stop them from guessing it was her. As he pictured the news making its way to Lizzie's ears, he noticed Tammy staring at him.

The certainty of the moment that just passed now quieted in the echo of "no."

When Rocky was a kid and he and his dad were hunting ducks at Lake Henry, a lake named for Henry Bomhoff whose farm it had been before a broken levy turned the black loam of his fields into a shallow, black lake, Rocky had dropped his father's best rifle into the lake's swampy edge not far from here. Lake Henry, while not deep, was known for its pilfering mud bottom that made boots disappear like sugar in hot tea. Rifles too, Rocky learned, after days of dredging. When he finally admitted that his dad's rifle was lost for good, he could tell by the furious bend of his father's eyebrows that he'd never make up for his mistake. Now, Tammy gave him the same hard look.

Tammy watched him push his hair back from his forehead in a gesture that, ten minutes earlier, she might have found endearing. Now she saw it was arrogant and heedless, despite the fact that his arms were extended toward her in a gesture that was both plaintive and defensive.

She turned her back to him and picked up her underpants from the oak sapling where they had landed, tossed gaily through the air minutes before in some manoeuvre Rocky had picked up from a movie, she now supposed. Pink with red lace trim, this was the first pair she had bought in the hope that someone would admire her in them. She and Lizzie—Lizzie!—had ventured into the pink excesses of the lingerie store for the first time last week to cap off an extravagant trip to the mainland during which they had spent their entire summer job earnings. The girls had run down the ferry's ramp to the bottom of the Leamington dock and leapt directly aboard the bus to Windsor, an additional forty-five minute drive that delivered them to the Devonshire Mall.

The Mall was better than a carnival. It was a brilliantly lit bacchanal of instant gratification for girls who did most of their shopping by catalogue. No more wondering for weeks over each purchase while it made its way through Canada Post. Would it fit? Were the colours right? Would the belt look like real leather? At the Mall, absolutely everything desirable could be tried on, argued over, abandoned for something else, purchased, and worn within the space of minutes, rather than weeks.

As she pulled her panties over her sneakers – she had already put her shoes on for some reason and she couldn't imagine removing them, tying, and untying them in front of him – she watched him think about what had happened.

"I'm sorry," he tried, "it just slipped out. Maybe because you're friends with her."

She knew – they both knew – that this statement, and everything he had said over the last months, was untrue. Rocky Ryerson wasn't "falling in love" with Tammy Preston. Just three months ago that would have been so completely unbelievable she would have laughed. But now, in the wistful grey moonlight, she saw how she had wanted to believe him and how he had wanted her to believe him.

It wasn't that he had done anything to trick her, he wanted to say. The excitement of her acquiescence, the rubbing against a soft body in the dark, the feel of his fingers curled around her true, plump breast were what he was falling in love with–not with Tammy herself, but with the sensations she availed.

Rocky loved Lizzie. At seventeen, he felt he moved between fourth and third on Lizzie's ordered list of might-loves, depending on how he cut his hair. He had no real chance to win her, but he stopped himself from knowing this.

Tammy loved Lizzie too, with the anguished warmth that ordinary girls love their meticulously gorgeous friends. It wasn't fair; it just was. And sometimes it was possible, Tammy thought, to hate the surface of something and love its contents, like a perfectly brewed tea in an ugly mug.

Lizzie's mug was flawless, that much was certain. Men from the mainland were known to sport a full, slack-jawed stare when she walked by. Women squinted at her from the corners of their wrenched-away eyes hoping to glimpse something that apologized for the rest: a wart, a weak chin, a wayward hair, a bulge of misplaced fat. There was nothing in her feature or figure to make a normal woman feel anything but landlocked in Lizzie's presence. Where other females walked, Lizzie sailed.

And yet she pulled everyone along in her wake, progressing steadily, a loyal presence who would yell at a mean boy for you or cry over a lost pet with you, or clap for joy at your small triumphs. She chose Tammy—the only other girl in first grade—to be her best friend ten years ago, and they were soaked in each other's lives ever since. Tammy's own mom thought Lizzie would end up a movie star, or prime minister, or maybe with her own talk show in Toronto. Lizzie didn't want to think that far ahead. She fretted about schoolwork and chores and fashion and her endless spiral of poems and diary entries and girlhood short stories, but not a future which, in the manner of all those born with beauty and intelligence and grace, she could look forward to without concern.

Rocky's love for Lizzie was layered. Her beauty was, in his eyes, proof of God's earthly reward, an outward reflection of inward splendor. His father had left them, pulling away from the island like an oil barge, angry and implacable, and Lizzie, unimaginably alert to his pain, had offered him comfort in the form of a poem. For *him,* he realized later with surprise bordering on electric shock; she'd written it specifically for *him,* to offer a way to think about things, she had said. She knew what it felt like, of course—her own father had split even earlier than his—but the fact that she thought of him long enough to write an actual poem took on its own meaning as the sharp memory of his father softened.

The day Ford Bicks first mentioned his new girlfriend was the day Rocky learned what despair felt like. Despair came to him like a commandment and immediately he was hunched over as if in pain. Despair, it turned out, wasn't a hyperbole. It was a physical sensation, something that started in your organs and radiated outward, burned you from the core, and left the rest of you numb.

Ford, Rocky could see, was aware of the damage he had inflicted in his overly casual announcement. Of course Ford would get Lizzie. He had made his way through all the young women of the island—the eligible and the not so eligible—as though training for the ultimate prize that he was now ready to claim.

"You raped me!" Tammy said, pulling the rug out from under his thoughts.

"What?" Rocky was startled, realizing what she meant. "Come *on*, Tammy."

"No, that was *rape*, by definition. No means *no*, remember?"

"Yeah, but you don't get to decide that afterwards. You don't get to say yes, then change your mind, eh? That's not how it works." He was trying to keep his voice down, keep the panic out. He didn't want to spook her into the unimaginable.

"I didn't say it after. I said it just as you were starting, and you didn't stop."

If he had gotten angry, if he had pleaded, if he had gotten up and pulled his truck away and not looked back, how would their lives have changed? Hers would be worse and his would be better, or so he thought.

Instead, he stayed and lied, and learned something new about fate and the conflicting pressures that pressed strength into character. He learned about love. He also learned a thing or two about his father.

Rocky looked at Tammy's tear-stained cheeks. She was pretty in her own quiet way. It wasn't fair that Lizzie's glowing presence cast shadows instead of light. It wasn't Tammy's fault she was plain by comparison. He knew this first hand. Crawford's mere proximity had turned Rocky himself into a loser, rather than an ordinary boy who tried and often failed.

Tammy sniffed, her nose full of tears, and wiped her cheek on her forearm. He stroked her back, half in sympathy, half in desperation.

"Don't do this. Please," he said.

"You don't love me! How could I be so stupid? You called me *Lizzie*! You wished I was *her*!"

That was when he saw how he and Tammy were meant to be. So he gave her a gift, the first of many, because maybe there was such a thing as a soul mate, and maybe you should keep them if you wanted them or not.

"What, you think I want Lizzie? You're kidding, eh? She's just so. . . *obvious*. All show. She thinks we're all fighting over her. It's stupid."

"Really?" Tammy wanted so badly for this to be true that she pretended to believe him.

And that's how things stood for the rest of her life, through three pregnancies and two daughters and eight jobs between the two of them.

They were as happy as most people get to be.

SWIMMING LESSONS

SWIMMING LESSONS

It sounded, we later agreed, like a deer was trying to burrow under the front porch. From the vegetable garden where I wrestled with deep-rooted dandelions, I could see the edges of the struggle. I shouted for my father to come, drawing the entire family from all edges of our property. They headed toward the commotion at different speeds, each according to their dispositions. My sister was the first to arrive, panting from a quick sprint. My little brother was second, his preferred locomotion a skip. My mother strode up next, removing her gardening gloves from her hands and tucking them into her belt. I fell in behind, shaking the dirt off my skirt and wiping my forehead with the back of my hand.

For years, our front porch had been the site of a pitched battle between Dad and the family of raccoons who thus far had dug through every barricade he had erected. But today's havoc was wreaked by something much larger than a raccoon. Whatever this was, it had managed to shift concrete pavers, pull away the trellis that had been nailed to an old masonry board, and even uproot the masonry board that had been dug in several feet underground. All had been tossed around like toys in a kid's room.

We took turns lying on our stomachs to peek through the debris and into the shadows under the porch. Two round golden eyes glowed back at us from the dark.

Fear didn't occur to us as we stood in the aftermath of the battle for the porch. No predatory animals had been spotted on the island in decades.

My dad was last to arrive, limping a little from the wrench he had dropped on his foot.

"What in hell?" He asked this question all the time, never expecting an answer. This time Mom supplied one.

"It's a dog, I think. Probably ran away from the hunt." Mom went inside and returned with a peeled boiled egg. She made kissing noises at the eyes. They blinked back at her.

"Come on, boy," she said. "It's okay. Come on, look, a treat!" The eyes focused on her, and a gentle, rhythmic whining issued forth. Mom could wheedle milk from a turkey.

Slowly, the outline of a dog—full chest, tapered waist and hound-dog head blackened by dirt—emerged from under the porch. Formal introductions were made, during which, still shivering, he politely sniffed hands all around. Then he shook his coat methodically, starting at his shoulders and ending with his tail, spraying us with earth. Taking the egg delicately from my mother's fingers, he strolled through the open door of our house without hesitation. We followed him into the kitchen and watched him settle on the braided rug in front of the sink. This would be his favourite spot for the rest of his life.

Physically, Ranger was the platonic ideal of his breed. His brown velvet ears, the saddle on his speckled coat, his brisk, cropped tail, his earnest expression—all were positioned and proportioned as though from a blueprint issued by the American Kennel Club. And he wasn't just a perfect physical specimen; he embodied the German shorthair pointer spirit, as well. At the barest hint of a bird's presence, his muscular body formed a perfect point, aimed at the precise location of his prey, and readied itself to launch into action at his master's command.

But at the gun's bark, instead of fetching, he fled. According to his breeder—a carefully dressed hunter who later tracked Ranger to our door—the dog had shown great promise until today. His bloodlines were immaculate, his training comprehensive. It was obvious from the way the hunter spoke that Ranger was once destined to be top dog in the man's award-winning kennel—the finest stud of a decades-long breeding program. And, moments before his headlong flight, Ranger seemed poised to fulfill his destiny. With clipped and bitter pride, the hunter described how the dog had quietly pointed to, then, on whistled command, flushed out a brace of pheasants in the confident manner of one born to the task. His owner took out two of the clutch in one shot. This part of the story was related in a way that was carefully not self-congratulatory, because the hunter's next command, "Fetch!" fell in empty air on the space where a dog used to be. At the rifle's crack, Ranger ran as though he himself had been shot from the gun. A few minutes and three miles later, he was cowering under our front porch, covered in dirt.

In the space of a single shotgun blast, Ranger had become a blight on his ancestry.

"There's not much you can do when a dog's born gun-shy," the man said. "I mean, when it happens by accident, like if someone stuck some birdshot in his butt, you might be able train it out of him." He lit the smoke he had pulled from a silver cigarette case. "But a dog like this—afraid his own shadow's going to bite him—well, there's not much you can do about that besides cull him."

My mother gasped aloud, giving voice to our collective concern. We all thought we had heard "kill him," which may, in fact, have been implied, but we never found out because our parents volunteered immediately to keep Ranger as a pet. In short order, they also promised to have him fixed and tell no one where we had gotten him. It was as though they were under some hypnotic spell cast by the hunter, or the dog, for that matter. And so, preempting the negotiations we pet-starved kids had been trying to open for years, Ranger was invited to live in the sanctuary where his flight from the gun had ended.

Before driving off in his oversized red pickup, the hunter asked Dad if he could have a last moment with the dog. Dad said yes, of course. As the man grabbed Ranger's collar and pulled him off a distance, we could all see it wasn't just guns the dog feared. The man seemed to be fondling Ranger's ear when the dog uttered two sharp yelps and pulled himself away to gallop back to our house.

When we gathered around Ranger, lounging on the now filthy braided rug, I saw that the AKC tattoo inside his ear had been replaced with a seeping burn, a fairly common approach for a kennel seeking to protect its reputation from a defective dog. There were worse ways, said Island lore. Everyone knew someone who had seen gun-shy dogs being flung from the island ferry some miles from shore.

We were murmuring over Ranger's poor ear when Mom noticed the lump in the side of his cheek. Gently, she lifted the flap of his jowl to reveal the egg she'd given him two hours before. He dropped it into her hand. It was perfectly intact, without so much as a tooth scratch marring its rubbery surface.

For me, the year Ranger arrived was a complicated one. I was fifteen years old and had begun to find a new purpose for the boys in my small world. I may have been a late bloomer but I was also a practical one, so I took stock of the options available within the confines of our little island in the middle of Lake Erie. My future, contained as it was within the thirty-four square miles of my world, seemed set in the island's bedrock.

That summer my unobtrusively flat chest burgeoned forth, making one boy awkward and shuffling, the next aggressive and forward, as though I'd grown breasts just to taunt them.

One night, to the lapping of the lake against the dock where we sat, I kissed Randy Jimson with a confused energy he mistook for invitation. An oddly polite, slow-motion struggle ensued. When I finally writhed free, I was left with semen on my jeans and a lasting sense of chagrin.

My best friend Stan, who had become one of the awkward and shuffling boys, became silent and angry after Randy and I kissed. Stan and I had spent many summers jumping into the hay in his uncle's barn, lounging around the island's one general store, fishing in a borrowed boat, or, when we had money to buy ammunition, engaged in target practice in a field. After the kiss, Stan was always too busy or too tired to hang out.

Randy called me repeatedly, having the impression that we were now "going together," but I brushed him off. Later he would tell everyone he ditched me because, sexually, I was both voracious and odd. Rumour is the primary news source in our small community, and the entirety of the island's population—which peaked at 150 during tourist season—had heard the broadcast within a week. While there was no overt unkindness in their musings, I could guess what was left unsaid in their neutral tones, their coolly framed, "Oh hello, Sarah." The false secret dogged me in the potluck serving line. Their raised eyebrows left Stan too busy to fish or swim or even, it seemed, to smile back at me.

As time passed, Ranger filled the space left by Stan.

He wasn't much of a conversationalist, but then, Stan hadn't been all that talkative either. Ranger and I walked for hours up and down the hedgerows, following his nose wherever it led us, unless it was hunting season. The moment Ranger heard gunshot, he would abandon me for his haven under the porch, running as though pursued by dog-eating demons.

Ranger wasn't just afraid of guns. Every single time my siblings and I went swimming, from the moment one of us was knee-deep in the lake until we were all back on dry land, Ranger would race back and forth along the length of the beach, barking continually, the duration of our swim measured by the hoarseness of his voice. Whether we were in the water for five minutes or two hours, Ranger never lost one iota of conviction that we were willfully endangering ourselves, and he was duty-bound to sound the alarm every second we remained in peril.

"What in hell is he doing?" We watched Dad's head swivel, his face incredulous, as he tracked Ranger's hysterical progress up and down the beach. From our various spots in the water we burst into laughter. This was the first time our father had witnessed what we called Ranger's Erie-o-phobia. We had grown accustomed to the dog's tenacious panic, but the expression on Dad's face renewed the hilarity. We enjoyed the dog's plight, and we'd egg him on every way we could think of. I would call him to me in my sweetest voice, my brother would throw sticks into the water for him to fetch, and my sister Kelly would shriek and flail and pretend to be pulled under.

Really, it didn't matter what we did. He behaved the same whether we splashed or floated. Ranger's fear wasn't caused by water. It came from inside him.

One afternoon, my dad called me in from my seat between the trellised rows in the vegetable garden where he believed I was picking and shelling peas for supper. I had finished with the peas an hour before and now Jane Austen was introducing me to Fitzwilliam Darcy's finer qualities. I closed my book and dawdled my way to the house. I had an idea what was coming.

"Sit down," Dad said in a formal voice, indicating the kitchen table. We had reached an awkward camaraderie over the years. He was a good father, patient and careful, and yet so unlike me it seemed we existed on different planes. He used to say he felt like a rooster trying to raise a duckling. We loved each other well enough to try to understand what the other said.

Mom was already sitting at the table, her eyes cast downward—guiltily, I decided—her finger idly tracing the lines in the butcher block.

"Your mother says you only applied to that one college. I thought you had put down three."

I had, but I knew they couldn't afford to send me to any of them. "Well, I'm not really interested in going away to college, Dad." Now *I* was the one staring hard at the table. "It's just not something I see myself spending four years on."

"Sarah," he said, pausing until I looked up at him. "Not everyone gets a chance to get a higher education. Me and your mum, for example, neither of us could have gotten in if we'd applied. But you've got a real chance to get your bachelor's degree. That's an important thing."

"But I don't need to study Liberal Arts if I'm only coming back to plan crop rotations."

Dad sat across from me for a silent eternity. "Now that I think about it, maybe you're right. We can't afford to pay tuition for you to study Arts when you're supposed to be managing the harvest. You can always read for fun." He was staring directly into my eyes. Although I knew he was being as direct as he could be, I still wasn't sure what I was supposed to do.

Ranger's "Terror on the Beach" routine was an almost daily occurrence that summer. Our favourite swimming spot was two minutes from our house. The thermometer was reaching new records, so we were there every second our days would allow. Freed both from the heat and gravity, I'd float on my back, slowly kicking back and forth, while Ranger, trapped onshore, kept up the alarm regardless of the temperature.

Oddly, Ranger always enjoyed the walk to the beach, never anticipating its purpose. He would bounce happily along, occasionally stopping to point at a pheasant peering out from behind a bush, then rushing at the bird with an innate efficiency that belied his sensitive side. Not once did he associate the bathing suits under our clothes, the towels over our arms, or even the rubber dingy Dad carried occasionally on his head with the terror of our immersion in the lake. He would lope along, oblivious, until the moment one of us was in the water, and that was it. Up and down the beach he would run, back and forth, never breaking stride, bellowing hysterically all the while.

"He's a total mental case. That's all there is to it." My brother's assessment may have been unkind, but it wasn't untrue. No one had ever heard of a dog that was afraid of the water. On the island, water was half of every landscape. Besides, dogs were expected to hold down more than one job. To be a companion was an important thing, but you still had to earn your keep. Ranger's only side project was killing the neighbour's chickens, a fact which did not endear him to Joe, the ancient curmudgeon who owned the farm next to ours. Joe made Mom pay top dollar for every mangled hen Ranger dropped so devotedly at her feet.

On a rainy day that July, as I walked down our hallway, my sister Kelly reached out and caught me by the arm. She looked both ways down the hall and then pulled me into her room. Placing a finger over her mouth, she peeked one last time out the door, then closed it and pulled me down to sit beside her on the frilly pink coverlet of her bed. I waited. She smiled broadly, gave a little squeal, and started flapping both arms at the elbows, her blonde curls bouncing in time.

"He asked me!" She finally said in a hissing squeal.

Kelly was my favourite person in the world. We had been communicating in shorthand since she was five and I was three. Things that took me ten minutes to relate to Dad I could tell her in three words.

In the three words she had uttered that day, she conveyed that John, her boyfriend of four years, had finally proposed and that she had accepted. They had set a date and were planning for four kids. She likely had ferry tickets in her purse for our trip to pick out her dress.

Seeing the expression on my face, she put both hands on her hips.

"Oh, stop it, Sarah! You be happy for me, starting right now!"

I didn't say anything. There was no point.

"I know, I know. You think I should move away, maybe live on the mainland for a while first. Explore all the options before I decide. But I don't need to do that. I just know."

"But how can you possibly 'just know'?" I said. "You've never been off the island more than a week in your life." My protest was uttered by rote; there was no chance she would listen, but *someone* in her life had to suggest investigating other options. And it wouldn't occur to anyone else but me.

The truth was that I had always pictured her a farmer's wife, her waist getting thicker, her cheeks rosier, and her curls tighter with each sensible haircut. The truth was also that she would be content that way.

All of this was in her quiet eyes as we sat there on the bed that day. So I recanted.

"I'm sorry," I said, fighting for sincerity. "John's a good guy. I know you'll be great together." She laughed, and her eyes grew moist, and I hugged her so she couldn't see that mine remained dry.

She held both my hands in hers and squeezed them for emphasis.

"Don't worry," she said. "You'll meet someone too, I just know it! I hear John's cousin is thinking of moving back to the island. He's really cute. Trust me, nobody in John's family would pay attention to anything coming out of Randy Jimson's mouth. That rumour isn't going to stick to you."

And that's how Randy's rumour circled back to roost. Of course my family knew. That was the moment I realized it. Now, my father's throat clearing, my brother's sidelong eye, my mother's pointed glance, my sister's worried smile all had the same meaning as Stan's granite silence. I thought I was protecting them all by feigning indifference, but the knowledge that they too had been affected by the rumour made me angry. As much as I couldn't imagine being trapped in the island's endless cycle of gossip, seeds, tractors, and combines, Kelly couldn't imagine anything else. So she pulled out the ferry schedule and we planned a trip to pick out dresses and flowers, while I forced myself to smile for her happiness.

Ranger never lost his fear of guns, but his fear of water was cured in about three minutes one very hot day that August. It was a typical afternoon and we were heading for our usual swimming spot. This time, though, we were accompanied by Spanks, an oversized, lumbering Black

Lab, lumpy and skinny in all the wrong spots. He wasn't a pretty dog, but he was as sweet as any you would ever meet. He was gentle and quiet, even with little kids and yappy dogs. And he was an excellent hunter, everyone said. Without hesitation he would crash through a crust of ice in duck season the moment the bird fell from the sky. He always came back with his prize, dropping it gently at his owner's feet, never leaving so much as a drop of saliva on the bird's unruffled feathers. Unlike Ranger, he would have been horrified at the idea of killing a defenceless chicken.

One of Spanks' primary responsibilities was to take lunch out to the fields where Bob, his owner, worked long hours to get the crops in. Bob's wife would say, "Take this to Daddy, Spanks; take it to Daddy," and she'd put the bag—containing all sorts of dog delicacies like cold cuts and cheese, along with the can of Pabst—on the floor. Spanks would just pick it up and let himself out, the screen door banging behind him. Brenda never even bothered to watch him leave. It didn't occur to her to worry that Spanks would steal "Daddy's" lunch for himself. He wouldn't.

This paragon of canine virtue accompanied us that late summer day. If I were a dog, I would have resented Spanks for setting the bar so impossibly high. As a human, I grew tired of hearing how easy Spanks was to train, how fearless and tireless and gentle he was. Every bit of carefully earned praise felt like an insult to my dog. And yet Spanks, for all his eager perfection, could not be less to blame.

Arriving at the shoreline, we lay our beach towels on some rocks in the sun and started mincing our way into the water. When Ranger loosed his first volley of hysterical barking, Spanks jumped to his feet and scanned the horizon, trying to determine where the menace from the water originated. No threat became apparent, so he joined Ranger's back and forth flight, barking at random intervals with the expression of one unsure whether it was time to applaud or if this was just a short pause in a long-winded aria. Ranger kept up the sound and fury, and eventually Spanks stopped following, sank his haunches to the sand and simply observed. As he watched, panting, his head moving back and forth like the audience at a slow-motion tennis match, Spanks' tongue hung out the side of his mouth. It was obvious he too was thinking, "What in hell?"

The big dog seemed content to observe for a while, but I guess he soon grew tired of the racket and it was an especially hot day for someone in a thick black coat so, casual as could be, he leapt into the water and swam toward us.

Observing this momentous act, Ranger cut off the alarm as abruptly as if he had been beheaded. He froze in place, his body rigid, watching Spanks with something like terrified awe. I think it had never before occurred to him that dogs, like humans, could be suicidal maniacs. Ranger stood there, transfixed, his eyes following Spanks as the big dog pushed himself determinedly through the water, stopping at each person to be patted and praised. Eventually, Spanks circled back to shore. He wasn't more than three feet from Ranger when he stopped and gave several mighty shakes, showering my dog with the droplets flying from his thick black coat. But Ranger didn't flinch. He just waited until Spanks was done, and then sniffed him all over, the Lab lifting limbs obligingly as Ranger contemplated the meaning of each scent.

Satisfied with his investigations, Ranger trotted to the water's edge, his gaze levelled on me. I called him. He stood very still for a moment and then, gathering himself, leapt into the lake as though tearing himself from the land. He bounded through the water until it was deep enough to swim and then kept coming toward me, his expression patient, unchanging. When he reached me, he paused long enough to wet my cheek with his nose, then turned and headed back to shore.

Later, when I ran shivering out of the water to throw a towel over my goose-pimpled shoulders, Ranger was lying on a rock, snoozing in the sun.

From then on, that's what he did whenever we swam.

As we returned to the house that afternoon, my mom ran toward us through the corn, waving an embossed envelope over her head. My father walked behind her, a strained smile pinching his face.

I'd won a scholarship to the college of my choice – a full ride, half a country away.

STAYING PUT

STAYING PUT

Here comes trouble. My wife's on the march, crossing the yard toward me like she's got orders to shoot to kill.

"Joseph Carter! What are you doing, cursing like that! Are you losing your mind?"

Mavis was a screecher when I married her, and not much has changed in that respect.

If I were the talking kind, I might tell her that the goddamn dog next door went and killed another of my chickens today. By all that's holy, if them neighbours don't keep that son-of-a-bitch Ranger out of my yard I am going to put some bird shot up his ass. Fleabag deserves a good shit-kicking, you ask me. Don't even hunt worth a damn—gun-shy as a damn quail. Only goes after birds stuck in a pen, and couldn't fly in the first place even if they wasn't. I should've grabbed my shotgun.

Mavis shakes her head and reminds me Jake's coming.

She's been a proper wife, I guess, but when she opens her mouth you just want to be somewhere else. After almost sixty years I'm not going anywhere, but that don't stop me wanting to.

She doesn't understand why I'm not more jacked up about Jake's visit. I guess it's about time Jake came back and I know I should be partially pleased about it, but I just ain't. At my age, I'm past being pleased about visits from a friend. Besides, Jake ain't really a friend. He's more like a used-to-be friend who carries my secrets around, as if he's the one gets to decide who to give them to.

I got the chores to finish up, anyway. Got some chicken shit to spread on the corn, and that barn door ain't going to paint itself. But just look at her, thumbs in her apron, mouth going a mile a minute. Woman's got stamina, gotta give her that. I'm just glad the new hearing aids came with a volume control.

I head back to the coop, turn my back on her while she's still yammering. Then I hear it, the sweetest sound on this island.

"Gramps? Gramps! Wait up!"

That there is my pride and joy, ponytail flying, coming in to help her Granddad with the chores. My Lizzie's an honest-to-God beauty. Curling blonde hair, sky blue eyes, and a sense of style she didn't get from her grandmother's side, that's for sure. She's wearing those short shorts Mavis gives her hell for, but if you got it, flaunt it, I says. And she's got it, all right. She's a good girl too, I don't care what anyone says. Sure, she likes the boys. They like her right back and as long as she's safe, it don't matter what else.

I never say this to nobody but her, but unless you know what's available in the world you just can't know what you want from it. If someone had told me that when I was young, my life would be different today. But it's the world that's different, now. Kids like Lizzie, they can do anything they want, be whatever they want, be *with* whoever they want—no restrictions. The opposite of how I've lived.

"This old wheelbarrow's on its last legs, eh, Gramps? It's about to rust right through."

"She's got one last run in 'er."

She nods and we work on, both quiet, filling that old barrow, when I remember that she's been coming in late.

"So," I says, "tell your old Grandpa what you been up to, nights." She's sweating a little from the effort of shovelling chicken shit, and there is no prettier thing than the little golden curls that form around her face when she's working hard. Yep. She's a good girl.

"Jimmy Tanner asked me out. Wants to take me to the mainland for the day—you know, movies and dinner—the works. He really likes me, and I kind of like him, and he's going to get the store and that big farm when his parents move to Florida. But. . . he's just not as sweet as Crawford Bicks. You know?"

Her eyes flicker to me, and I hang on to them with mine.

"Yep," I says.

"I know Crawford's not the best choice for my future, but he's so sweet to me, Gramps, you'll see. He's one of the good guys."

Now she's leaning on her hoe, all dreamy-eyed—*Craw*ford this and *Craw*ford that—and that's when I truly realize she's going to marry someone and leave us, some day. We lost her mama long enough ago that the ache is numbed by time, but it will never be anything but pain. Sure, Lizzie's happy, but I'm worried. I have always been the only man in her life—her own daddy seen to that—and I never, until this moment, thought someone else could take my place. But look at those eyes, watching something far away heading toward her.

"You know what Crawford did, Gramps?"

And we're off.

"He took me out on his boat last night and he said 'Shhhh, listen' and we were quiet for a bit. He wanted me to hear the water splashing the hull. I never noticed what a pretty sound that was until then."

See why I love this child?

"It's funny, eh Gramps, growing up around water—the things you don't notice about it? Crawford said it's a song the lake sings to the boat. Isn't that crazy romantic?"

It is—I ain't gonna lie. And that Ford Bicks, well, he *is* a good looking boy. Tall and straight, with good, muscular arms. Like all of them, he's over the moon about my Lizzie. One of them Jimson boys wouldn't stop coming around for a while either. But as I was saying, she's got her pick of the litter. Even the girls love her. Hell, she could marry one of *them*, if she wanted, like that Ellen on TV. World's her goddamn oyster. Wasn't like that in my day. No sir, no how.

"Gramps, Mavis told me you were having a visit from an old friend. Who is it?"

"Don't go callin' grandma by her first name, now. They'll be hell to pay."

"It's okay, I only do it around you. But I'm not being rude. It's a mark of respect," she says, her dear, serious face making it true.

"Oh, you don't respect your old granddad?" I says, coaxing.

"I love my Gramps! You know that!"

"Oh yeah? Well then prove it."

This is how I usually earn a big fat kiss on the cheek to smile about the rest of the day. I've been eighty-two years on this earth, almost, and those wet smacks on my cheek offer my only real opportunities for joy. I take it where I can get it.

"But who's the old friend, Gramps? I was thinking about it and I've never known you to have any visitors from the mainland."

Oh boy, here we go.

"No one you know. Go grab a hoe. Help me get started weeding the corn."

Jake's family sold the farm and moved to the mainland when we was sixteen. Haven't seen him since, but he drops me a line once in a while. He went to the university, and travelled around some, and now he's settled down in Windsor. He was a bigwig up at Heinz, at one time. Likely retired, now.

Anyways, Jake's decided to join the pheasant hunt this year, and asked if he could stay with Mavis and me. It's an odd thing, considering that most days the only person who walks in our door besides the two of us is Lizzie. But it's okay. They say a change is as good as a rest. I guess.

"Grandma told me that you were really good friends with this Jake guy when you were young." Lizzie's looking into my face, trying to read my mind. "I get the feeling she doesn't approve, eh?"

Young lady is just as sharp as a fox in a corner. Can't hide a thing from her.

"Well, she don't approve of much, far as that goes," I says.

"True." She stops mixing chicken shit into the ground around the corn and looks me right in the eye as she is liable to do. "But neither do you."

"No more back talk from you, now! We got to get this watered in before the sun gets too high."

She gives a little chuckle, as though she got me good, and we work in sweet silence for the rest of the hour.

Later on, I decide to go have a little talk with Mavis regarding her running off at the mouth. She's sitting in her "library," she calls it, though it's like me calling the vegetable garden a factory farm. I built the damn thing for her, and still I can't stand to come in here. All four walls are covered, floor to ceiling, with bookcases stacked with her Harlequin Romances, four deep.

I swear there are tens of thousands of romances in this room alone, and that don't count the dozen or so boxes in the attic. Woman does nothing else, it seems, besides cook and clean and read these trashy books. I've read a couple myself, enough to know every goddamn one is exactly the same. She's like those people on that TV show, *Hoarders*, except instead of cats or newspapers, she's got shitty books. It's an embarrassment, but she says if I took better care of her, she wouldn't need them. Fair enough. But she has no business coming between me and my grandchild, and I'm here to remind her of that fact.

"Why'd you go telling Lizzie that Jake's coming, old woman?"

"What do you care, Joe? He *is* coming, isn't he? Got something to hide?"

"I ain't got nothing to hide! God*damn* it! You treat everything like it's got some hidden meaning and you're the only one can see it."

"Really? Are you saying that Jake coming back after all of these years doesn't have any kind of special meaning, Joe?"

So help me, I hate her some days, I really do, in her old grey dress and perpetual frown and that god-awful apron. She has been the bane of my existence since she first started making eyes at me in tenth grade. Looking back, I figure she had set her mind on me when we was in first grade at the island school. For years she just bided her time, waited till the other girls had given up, found someone else or moved all the way to the mainland to find somebody.

Nobody ever caught Jake's eye, which was one reason his parents moved away, I suppose. Not for want of girls trying, though. Everyone considered Jake a catch, and not because his family was rich – they wasn't – or his looks was good – they was – but because even as a boy, he was the kind everyone wanted to be around. He had that integrity; he could look you in the eye and tell you exactly how things were.

Jake was wise beyond his years and he made you feel *you* were wise, too. Once we sat on the west dock, our feet in the water while the sun dropped behind the waves, and talked for hours about everything you could imagine, and I spilled my guts and so did he.

I have always remembered what he said to me that night. Sometimes I wake up and it's at the tip of my tongue.

"Joey," he said, "I refuse to live by rules that were designed to prove I don't exist."

It was the kind of night you don't feel lucky for until you realize it ain't going to happen again. Never. If I had known, maybe I would have tried a little harder. When I put my hand on his thigh, maybe I would have kept it there a little longer. Who knows—maybe it wasn't that he didn't feel the same about me.

Anyway, most people can't live too far from everyone's expectations of them. I sure couldn't. Still to this day, when I imagine coming clean, I picture my good-for-nothing daddy's face. He's been dead over thirty years, and I can still see his hateful suspicion, like an accusation before the crime.

Around the time Jake's family moved off the island, Mavis came to me to say that she didn't mind I wasn't the romancing type. She just wanted a good provider, and I could be that for her. And I was. But in most of my eighty-two years, no one has ever, and I mean never, provided for me. I got everything I own by the skin of *my* teeth.

Fact is, my daddy almost lost the farm by the time I was twenty. He'd been showing off for years buying equipment the land couldn't pay for. Spent *his* daddy's inheritance on a combine harvester that was too heavy for our soil. I had to work day and night to put the finances right again while that piece of crap sat rusting in the barn.

Point is, I have never done nothing for myself alone.

I always done for other people—what they wanted of me, what they expected of me—and denied everything to myself. There's a lot of regret in that. Eighty-two years, so far.

And now, here we wait at the north dock, Mavis and Lizzie and me, for the ferry to show. The autumn sun is sharp in the sky, making Lake Erie a harder shade of grey. Finally the Pelee Islander comes chugging up from the distance, fifteen minutes late, like clockwork. I'll be calling that boneheaded Fred Pierce to remind him I said the new route was going to be longer, and they're going to have to change the schedule. I'm going over this conversation in my head and I forget why we're here until Mavis elbows me, chasing the frown off my face.

The big old ferry pulls up to the wharf and the deckhands make ready with their ropes. I can see Jake on the upper deck and even from down here I can see he hasn't changed much. His hair's all white, but he's still got some. Not like me.

Jake waves both hands at us like he's flagging down a car, and I smile and wave right back. Then I notice Lizzie looking at me, her head to the side, a little smile stuck on her own face like she'd forgot to remove it. Mavis, of course, has her lips pursed, but Mavis always has her lips pursed, like she was born holding her teeth in.

"Well doesn't he look like a proper gentleman?" Mavis says and she's right, but why does she have to be so bitter all the goddamn time? Nothing wrong with taking care of your appearance. Although she'd never know it.

Sure enough, Jake comes stepping toward us off the ramp, wearing a brown tweed jacket with those leather elbow patches. Looks like he belongs on the pages of that gentleman's hunting quarterly I saw in the Treasurer's Office last time I paid my taxes. He's got a German shorthair pointer—identical to that brainless mutt that's been killing my chickens—and it's marching toward us like it owns Jake, the ferry, all of the island, and us.

Next thing, Jake's kissing my rigid wife and holding my granddaughter by the elbows to get a look at that face and then he's hugging me—*hugging* me and I don't know whether to hug back or squirm away so I do a bit of both. And then we three get in the cab of the pick-up, leaving Lizzie to bounce around in the truck bed with the dog, like she did when she was little, and Jake and Mavis are making small talk as if all this were a normal thing.

Back at home, Lizzie and Jake go at it like two little old ladies, laughing at celebrity news on the TV and gossiping about the locals. Turns out Jake's been in touch with a lot of people over the years. He knows more about everyone's business than Mavis. So of course Mavis joins right in and I'm the odd man out for a while, but for some reason, I'm feeling the way I do right after Lizzie kisses my cheek. I listen to them all go on, and I'm *still* smiling and feel no need to stop.

Too soon, Mavis is getting Jake settled into the spare room where I usually sleep—me and her and Lizzie having somehow, silently, agreed to pretend I usually sleep with my wife. I'm changing into my pajamas in the bathroom, and making my slow way toward my wife's bed, my movements awkward, her back lined up against me.

"Good night," I say.

"What?" She can't believe I have anything to say to her, and truth be told, neither can I.

"Good night," I say again. It's not really her fault. It's never been her fault. She's tried but she can't never be right. And how can I expect her to?

Next thing I know, the alarm clock's ringing. It's 4:30 am and before my eyes open, a smile is squeezing my face. Pretty soon Jake and I are in the kitchen, Mavis putting coffees in our hands and bacon and eggs on our plates. We throw our orange vests over our hunting jackets, fill our pockets with shells, sling shotguns over our shoulders, and head out the back door to hunt along the hedgerow between my house and the neighbours' place.

Now, if you ain't never seen a ring-neck pheasant, you are really missing something special. The males are one of the prettiest game fowl you'll ever lay eyes on. They've got these iridescent green heads with a long crest out behind and big round eye patches with bright red skin like the wattle on a chicken. Their long, striped tail feathers drag the ground behind them when they're walking. In the air, their tails spread out like a long, pointed fan. A pheasant in flight is truly something to see. They're pretty good on the table, too—if they're done right—all juicy breast meat just gamey enough so you can tell the difference from chicken.

But Jake don't care if we bag one, I can tell, so we let the dog point and flush where she may, and we set up on a felled tree to pass the thermos of coffee and Canadian Club back and forth. The fields, the grass, the hedgerow—everything's the same colour beige, like straw that's been in the sun too long. The guns of the other hunters are going off in random bursts like popcorn in a fire, loud but at a comfortable distance. The sky is the darkest shade of blue. For some reason, that's what stuck in my head—the exact colour the sky was when Jake decides to throw the bomb.

"So, you seem well, Joe," he says, and I don't know whether he means it, if all the grinning I've been doing since he's been here makes me seem it, but I decide to go along.

"Yep," I say. "Doing pretty good."

"Are you, then? Really?"

"Yep," I say.

"Well, so am I. That's one of the reasons I'm here, actually."

I stiffen and I don't even know why.

"I wanted you to be the first person from home that I told." He's reaching his hand over to put it on my shoulder and I'm liking this less and less.

"Joey," he says, "I'm in love. At almost eighty years old, I am finally, truly in love, and I'm planning to get married."

What the fuck, I wonder but don't say. I just look at him, waiting.

"His name's Chuck. Well, most people call him Charles but I know you'd insist on calling him Chuck. He used to teach Economics at the University of Windsor. He's retired too and we plan to spend the rest of our lives travelling together."

Suddenly I feel like the wind's going to knock me right down. I sit, but he goes on a little faster as though he just wants to fit this last part in.

"I'd be very happy—that is *we'd* be happy—to have you at our wedding. You and Mavis. And your lovely Lizzie, for that matter. If you'd come. It's a special occasion, two old bachelors finding love. A rare event."

He's looking up at me, as if all this wasn't a dirty joke to play on an old geezer with a heart condition. And to remind me, my heart is pounding and my mouth is dry. My left arm even aches.

"What in hell are you talking about, Jake?" I feel like I'm saying the words too slow, like I've got to force them out of me. "A man? You're marrying a man for God's sake? At your age? Jesus H. Christ!"

God knows why he seems surprised. Now he's the one who's waiting.

"I mean, it's disgusting," I say, while I'm really just working on *what* to say, what's expected in a situation like this, and I come out with the obvious. "It's disgusting and it puts my marriage to shame. My normal marriage—to shame! I'm going to be sick to my stomach!"

But I don't want to be sick to my stomach. I'm feeling something else, something that don't bear thinking about. Something forlorn and angry.

His face is sagging, deflated like a kid's day-old balloon.

"So that's how you've decided to react, Joe?" He's looking right at me, won't take his eyes away, as though *he's* got a leg to stand on here. "Because I'm certain you wouldn't have felt this way when we were sixteen." His voice is low, and to me, it sounds like a threat.

I grab my 12 gauge from where it's leaning up against a tree and cradle it in my arms, not exactly pointing it at him, but not pointing it the other way, neither. Joe stands, too. He looks worried, and so he should. You don't tell another grown man a thing like that and expect it to be all happy days from then on in. I stare into his face, then spit on the ground at his feet. I turn and head for my regular home and my regular marriage, hoping the natural way of my life will drive this unwelcome sorrow out of me and right back to hell where it belongs.

I never see Jake again. He rents a cottage on the east side for the rest of the hunt, and I keep to myself as much as possible until he leaves. The day he shows up to get his stuff, I'm staying in Mavis' room, waiting for him to leave. Hiding, really. I hear his footsteps in the hallway, then he knocks on the door, saying my name a couple times while I'm shaking my head and keeping my mouth shut. I've got Daddy's Smith and Wesson in pieces on an old towel beside me on the bed. Whenever I get to feeling like this, I clean Daddy's gun. Lately, I've been doing it a lot.

"I'm sorry," he says in an almost-whisper from the other side of the door, and he's gone.

After Jake leaves Pelee, everything changes. Ford Bicks, it turns out, has his own ideas about the future and he goes and applies to the University of Windsor. Next thing we know, Lizzie's on her way to the big city, too. I miss her something fierce and I worry, because it's just so goddamn sudden. She and Ford sometimes make the trip back out, but it's never the same. Also, I don't know Ford Bicks real well, and maybe I expected she'd always need her old granddad to protect her. I figured she'd always be around, helping with the chores, waiting for me to coax one of those sweet kisses to my wrinkled old cheek. I guess I figured wrong. I'm a foolish old man, that much is obvious.

But I'm managing. It all would of been A-OK, except that damn Mavis can't stop from being a gossip.

"What?" she keeps saying, "what happened with Jake?"

in a voice like a horse demanding hay, and she will not let it go. So after a while, I tell her about the "wedding" invitation just to shut her up and maybe enjoy the look on her face.

What surprises me is that she is not surprised. She's not surprised but there's something else on her face, something sharp and pained and spiteful.

"Oh yeah," she says, "Lizzie called that one."

"Wait, Lizzie what now?" I say because I need to get some time to think before Mavis says the next thing.

"Lizzie called it. Lizzie told me Jake was gay that first night he was here. Says she's got the 'gay-dar' and that she could tell he was one of them when we picked him up from the boat. Says she's surprised you didn't know, since you were friends so long. I didn't tell her what good friends you were, though. I spared her that because she doesn't need to know her own grandpa is some kind of goddamn queer who only married me so he could hide it. But maybe she deserves to know! Maybe she'd want to know her perfect grampa is just a miserable old faggot."

But I ain't no faggot. I never done nothing—never done nothing at all. I might've thought about things to do, but I never done them. Jake's the only one knows that, though. Thinking about a thing and doing a thing, they're not the same at all. Mavis, with her thousands of romances, ought to know the goddamn difference.

She's still yammering on as I go unlock the cabinet and pull out Daddy's old Smith and Wesson. It's loaded—I keep it that way—and I look her in the eyes. She stops and stares at me like I'm already a ghost and I stick that thing in my mouth and I'm about to pull the trigger when a familiar commotion starts up in the yard.

I look out the window and it's that goddamn dog driving my chickens from one side of the coop to the other in bursts of frenzied squawking. I go down the stairs as fast as my tired old legs will carry me, and when I finally make it down to the yard feathers are floating and that bastard's got my fattest Leghorn by the neck and two others dead on the ground.

He's occupied with the bird flapping around his eyes so he don't see me until I'm a couple feet away and then bang! bang! bang! I unload Daddy's gun right through that bird and into the dog's head.

COMING BACK ALONE

COMING BACK ALONE

I've been walking for hours, my now useless left foot leaving a punctuated blood trail in the thankless ice. I climb the rocks to the shore, stumbling to escape the frozen lake. Lights from my mother's house, blanketed with new snow, glow in the dimming sky. It's not a comforting sight.

I limp through the door, greeted by the struck faces of my mom and nieces and daughters – and Lizzie my sweet wife – and all I can hear is that song that goes, "Today is the first day of the rest of my life" as though something like that must always be a good thing, when now I know it's not.

"My God, Crawford!" my mom is almost screaming, and for once melodrama is not unjustified. "Thank God!" She says, gasps through tears and shoves people aside to get at me. "What happened?" she asks, but she's not waiting for answers. "We thought you were lost! We thought you were dead!" She hugs me, her little fists fierce in the small of my back, her face scrunched into the middle of my chest. She sobs, for real, and I know what comes next, everyone must.

"Where's Rocky? What happened to Rocky?" I push myself away and head toward my old room upstairs. "Crawford! Crawford Bicks!" Her voice recedes as I slam the door and lock it, leaving them all crowded in the front room amongst the doilies and Royal Doulton figurines.

Fully clothed, still soaking wet, I lay on my boyhood single bed, my room covered in pennants and Pink Floyd posters, just the way I left it, and I shiver.

Me and Rocky have been best friends for years, each other's best and worst influence since we started making money on the Tooth Fairy. Once, when we were seven, we ran away from home together. Rocky's dad—my uncle Carl—had spanked Rocky so hard he had bruises all over his ass. Rocky decided to run away, so I figured I'd join him.

"Mom, can you make us a sandwich?" I said, wheedling. Never hit the road on an empty stomach was a rule she had taught me and, at seven, it was a piece of advice I was prepared to accept.

"Not now. Can't you see I'm busy?" Mom was the island's secretary treasurer, and she was always fiddling with paperwork, either on the kitchen table so she could look after me, or in her office over at the Town Hall next door. At the moment, our kitchen table was covered with ledgers and pens and a ruler. And Mom was wearing those cat eye glasses, a sure sign she meant business.

"Please Mom! Rocky's hungry and we need to run away." Mom always had a sweet spot for Rocky, and he loved her back with a shy wistfulness that was sad to me, even when I was seven. He used to bring his treasures to her, make gifts of them, like the egg-shaped rock he had found that she still, today, displays on her dresser. So it was never a bad idea to bring him up when I wanted something. I put my hand on Rocky's shoulder and looked into Mom's eyes.

"Please?"

Her face twisted as she looked at him and I watched as she noted his tear-stained face, the way he sat so gingerly in his chair. She sighed, touched his cheek, and went to the pantry for the bread. She had us all packed up with our food in kerchiefs tied on the ends of sticks—weird setup if you asked us, but she didn't—then made us wait at the door while she ran for the Instamatic.

"Okay, smile!" she said, snapping a few shots. "You guys are so cute I can hardly stand it." She sent us on our way, her face flickering between a smile and something more complicated.

We made it to the top of the island that day, two seven-year-olds, proud and tired and dusty from four miles of gravel road. But when we got to the north dock we didn't know what to do after that. So we went up to Dockmaster Fred Pierce, and he called my mom to come get us.

I don't know what happened to Rocky that night. Likely nothing. His mom was in bed most of the time. Much later, I came to the conclusion that my aunt had suffered from high-grade depression all her life. As I recall, Uncle Carl was either furious or unnervingly jubilant. They both had a short memory when it came to parenting, though. That's how things were at my cousin's house. Down, down, down or up, up, up. That was the only constant.

One of the constants in my life was Rocky. When we were nine, playing in a hedgerow beside a frozen corn field, the dried yellow stalks poking out like broken bones from rows of frozen earth, I fell from a tree and fractured my wrist. Rocky pulled me home on the sled we'd brought, both of us crying the entire three miles of busted ground. He let me squeeze his hand white while René, the nurse who comprised the entirety of the island's medical community, cast my arm so I could be flown to the mainland. Rocky never stopped crying until I did. Mom let him sleep over, and I woke up to the sound of him sobbing in his sleep. The thing of it is, he was never much of a crier, otherwise.

When we were two of only six eleventh-graders at the island high school, Rocky and I had a falling out.

A bad one. I had good grades, the baseball team, and Lizzie, whom Rocky had always, pseudo-secretly, loved. His love for her had never been a secret to me, of course. But I couldn't very well stop myself from pursuing her just because Rocky wanted another thing he couldn't have.

So I had Lizzie, and all these other things, while Rocky had booze, bad grades, and thievery—not a good idea on an island with a total population of the mainland high school. It was sad, but as my mom said, neither was it unexpected. Although she pursed her lips over Rocky for years, she always kept a place for him in our home and in her heart.

I don't know what it was that set him off. Maybe it was this: we were sitting in the Jimson's hayloft on a warm Saturday in spring, smoking—him and Lizzie and I—when I reached over and caught her hand and kissed it.

First I should explain that Lizzie is the most beautiful girl anywhere, not just on the island. She's all legs and eyelashes and smooth hair and sweet, sweet smile and sometimes the guys would marvel that she lived here at all. Her being mine, though, felt right. Maybe Rocky didn't think so.

Anyway, as I grabbed her hand and kissed it that day, Rocky jumped up and said we should go explore the tourist cottages. This was something we had done fairly often as kids, but when you start to understand the nature of consequences, well, it just stopped seeming like a good idea. I guess guilt made me go along. It would be just another regretful incident to add to the rosary of bad ideas strung by Rocky.

"Crawford." I loved the way Lizzie started using my full name the moment she was mine, and never once before. Everyone besides my mother has always called me Ford. "Crawford," she said, trying not to say it in a way that made Rocky think she was wearing the pants, but coming across that way nonetheless. "You're not really going, are you? Bad idea."

I couldn't very well have a girl tell me what to do, not even Lizzie, and certainly not in front of Rocky, so that pretty much confirmed my participation in the whole ill-fated ordeal. I gave her a bald look and just laughed in the manner of all superior males when yanked on by their uppity girlfriends. I think she got it because she dropped the lecture.

So Rocky and I jumped down from the loft into the pile of hay below, while she sat there, smoking and shaking her head. Later Don Jimson would call our parents to give us shit for smoking in his barn but, as trouble went, it got kind of buried in the real mountain of shit we found ourselves under that day.

See, when Rocky was angry, he never showed it in his face, or even in his actions in a normal way. I never saw him yell. He never got into a fight. His anger always seemed to turn inward. Whatever he did would hurt him more than anyone else, like the scratch marks he made on his inner arms. He said doing it calmed him down. You never really knew with Rocky, until it was too late and then, boom.

The tourist cottages were mostly on the south shore. It tends to flood down there, so it's useless for farming and the best hunting is also inland. Island folk don't feel the need to live on the water, I guess. We already know we're surrounded.

I let Rocky drive my old Ford pickup, my way of making up for Lizzie, I suppose, and he headed right for the rich people's places—the ones with docks on the water and trampolines in the yard. They had the coolest stuff to sift through, and they were only there in the summer. Tourists were transients, practically translucent compared to real Islanders. Mostly they were thin, fit, academic-looking types, dads who played tennis or tanned, stay-at-home moms in expensive fitness wear with tidy little kids in tow. Even if you didn't already know everyone on the island by first and last name, you'd see right away these people didn't belong. The gnarled farmers in their suspenders and straw hats, the weathered fishermen in their perpetual stink and hip waders, even we island kids with our outdated clothes and casual independence—we all gave the tourists a wide berth, especially the ladies. They'd step up to Jon Tanner, owner of the general store, and ask for things like sprouted bread and avocados as though it didn't take a major effort just to keep us islanders in regular food.

I'm digressing, I guess, because this memory really bothers me.

Rocky pulled up beside this one cottage, hiding the truck more or less behind a big clump of forsythia, the spray of yellow flowers something we would have collected for my mom in earlier days, and grabbed a crowbar out of the bed. Believe it or don't, this didn't seem ominous at the time, just practical, so I hopped out and followed him to the back door. He popped off the door handle like he was pulling the cap off a beer bottle and the door swung open, easy peasy. You could see right away these cottagers had an artistic streak, with their high, whitewashed walls, yellow shag rug and paintings of sunflowers. The unfinished sunflowers on a canvas in the corner proved the artist who had painted them lived here. That work in progress didn't tip us off to the cottage being occupied, though. To us it just seemed like the show-offy kind of thing tourists would leave around to gather dust over the winter.

We started going through their stuff, just checking it out, really, books on Van Gogh and intricate wooden puzzles and board games – the things tourists buy to make their leisure time bearable – me leaving things more or less as I found them, Rocky rifling through all haphazard and making a noticeable mess.

"Hey, cut it out," I said. "Put it back the way you found it. You trying to get us caught?"

"What the fuck Ford? Why you always such a pussy? Don't get your panties in a bunch." This was the tricky thing about always being superior to Rocky – and I'm just being honest because I know it's what's called for – I really couldn't be a pussy in his vicinity. So I backed off. I always backed off. I should have known that someday things would get to the point when it would be too late to back out. Like they did that day.

And now Lizzie calls through the keyhole of my locked bedroom door and I'm crying again, remembering. I can hear the crowd downstairs getting louder and yet quieter, as though whispering at the top of its voice.

So as Rocky threw things around, I tried to kind of keep the mess he made contained, surreptitiously flipping through each book he tossed on the floor for a moment before placing it back on the shelf. To be honest, I had always held him back from disaster with a prim self-satisfaction. But not anymore.

I remember he suddenly got real quiet for a moment before he called out "Bingo." He held up this wedding ring he took from a fancy wooden box with a rose carved into the top. The ring was old-fashioned and kind of tarnished, with a gigantic diamond jutting out like an afterthought. It looked like something a rich grandmother would wear. Rocky turned it to catch the light coming in from the floor-to-ceiling windows, and that's when we heard it. A footstep, quiet and shy, like someone backing out of the room. Rocky leapt to his feet, crowbar in hand, and stepped toward the sound.

There was a shriek, and Mrs. Mcready—whom I now recognized as the pain-in-the-ass cottager who hassled mom at the town hall, bitching about her taxes—was staring at us, terror in her eyes. I knew he'd never use the crowbar—to this day I know he would never have used it—but Rocky was holding it like a weapon over the head of this small, thin old lady whose bones might shatter if you looked at them too hard. She screamed again.

I grabbed Rocky's arm to pull him out the door but he stopped and turned and paused a moment, then whipped that ring at her chest from three feet away.

It bounced off and landed ringing on the ground. She screamed again and we ran to the pickup. I revved it as I drove away, my new tires pulling up the grass, leaving unmistakable tracks in the ground.

As the storm died down, Rocky was sent to reform school on the mainland and I was shipped off to college. Mrs. Mcready, a difficult woman, as my mother called her, and a goddamn fucking bitch, as Rocky called her, told the whole story more or less accurately, but making me out to be the hero of the day. I imagine the island cop, Blake Irvine, shook his head when she described Rocky's part, and nodded when she described mine. I'd been on his baseball team since I was twelve, and Rocky had been on his shit list for approximately the same length of time. When Blake showed up at my door, he let mom fix him a cup of coffee while he lectured me about using my head. When he showed up at Rocky's door, he brought handcuffs.

Mom is with Lizzie at the door now. Their knocks are getting more insistent, and I know leaving them out there is unkind of me. I also know I need to get René to have a look at my black foot, but I can't seem to get up. I guess

I'm afraid if I leave my too-small bed, I will make it all turn real. Stupid, I know, but sometimes the mind works in ways that make reality easier to bear. I just need a little while longer. No one would begrudge me that.

Don't get me wrong, Rocky didn't spend his whole life bouncing around reform schools, as stories like these often go. It took him about a year to get reformed, then he came home and took a job as a deckhand on the ferry. Being a deckhand on the ferry was a pretty important job, as island life went, respectable even. Pelee Island is a nine by four-mile oblong in the middle of the west corner of Lake Erie with two finger-like projections, one that points north, toward Canada, and another that points south toward the US. Besides a tiny airport that caters to expensive charter planes, the ferry is the only connection to the mainland. There are actually two ferries that run from spring to fall—one to Leamington, Ontario and one to Sandusky, Ohio.

I phoned him once when I was home on summer break, but my aunt said Rocky wasn't available. Her tone was uncharacteristically formal, so I didn't try again.

A few years later, though, home on another break, I ran into Rocky at the island tavern, hanging around with the other guys who had never left. He bought me a beer, I bought him a few, and we laughed and talked until the intervening years disappeared. Even though I didn't live there anymore, we never lost touch after that. I would call him when I knew I was coming to visit, and we would hang around in the ferry's engine room, earphones blocking out the noise and the need for conversation, while I watched him take pride in his work.

I married Lizzie and took her away with me to Windsor, and Rocky married Tammy, a distant second best. He worked his way up to ferry engineer, and I became a computer programmer. We bought houses, mine nice, his mediocre, had two daughters each, mine nice, his difficult—although I've always had a soft spot for his girls—and we lived our lives fairly well, I'd say. We both stayed married, until Tammy died. She had the same breast cancer that took down her mother and her grandmother and, like them, she simply left it too late. It was about then that Rocky started to take drinking more seriously, and not a soul could blame him.

Someone tries to push the door open and Mom's tone is more insistent. "Crawford, please! We've got search parties all over the lake! Where is Rocky? Are you bleeding? You left a trail all the way up the stairs. Crawford, honey, please open the door."

She is almost wailing, but softly, so I pull the pillow over my ears, and her voice becomes a murmur. It's okay for a while.

Last week, I brought the family home for the kids' March break, flying us over on the island's charter service. On a cold, sunny Wednesday afternoon, yesterday, in fact, Rocky and I powered up his snowmobiles and headed to the tavern for old time's sake. When we got there, Rick Baker was locking the place up.

"What's going on, Rick? I've never seen this place closed," Rocky said. I knew that meant it never did close because he was always either there, or on the ferry.

"We're all out, if you can believe it," said Rick, shaking his head as though he himself found it hard to believe. "The last shipment never came from the mainland. Even the liquor store is dry, eh?"

"You got to be fucking kidding me!" Rocky's face indicated that this was a life or death problem. We had chugged his last two beers while we donned our snowsuits.

"Yeah, well, it's winter. If the planes don't fly, we're shit out of luck. I just hope Jon doesn't run out of baby formula—then I'll really be fucked."

"What are you talking about? We're fucked now!" Rocky said. "The next shipment isn't until next week!"

"Well, I'm hoping to get something sooner, but Dave hasn't promised, and I'm not paying a ninety-buck premium to charter in a couple two-fours. It ain't worth it." Rick wrapped his scarf around his neck and walked to his car, while Rocky stood there, gaping. Then he turned to me, and I saw him formulating what turned out to be his second worst idea ever.

"Let's go across on the snowmobiles."

"What? Are you crazy?" I asked, but was already thinking it might be a cool idea. People used to make the 17-mile trek to the mainland all the time. We never had, though. It could be dangerous, but the weather was fine, and the lake had been frozen solid for a while.

"What's crazy about it? We'll be careful. Let's take the trailer and bring back enough to last us a while. Maybe I'll even make a profit—charge Rick a premium."

I stood there, my snowmobile helmet in my hand, uncertain. I just needed a final push.

"Crawford Bicks, come on down! Live a little, for fuck's sake."

Put like that, how could I refuse? I wish I had, but I didn't.

We went back to Rocky's and hooked up the trailer over Lizzie's weak protestations—another dynamic that hasn't changed much—and we headed across the lake.

Five hours later, we had a trailer full of beer and stomachs full of stew. We even got three big cans of baby formula, mainly to mock Rick. Turns out Rocky had more than one drinking place, and the girls in this Leamington bar knew him well from those days when the ferry has a long stopover. I was on my second beer and Rocky on his sixth or seventh whiskey when one of the girls, the pretty one who rightly treated us like middle-aged losers, told us the weather was getting worse.

"Not like, blizzard bad, but, like, you-don't-want-to-be-caught-out-in-the-middle-of-Lake-Erie bad," she said.

"Okay," Rocky said, and came up with the last, worst idea of his entire life. "Set me another couple of shots and we'll head out."

And now I'm curled up on my childhood bed with a pillow wrapped around my head and my foot shrieking like bloody hell while my entire extended family pounds on my door and my body rocks and shivers and tears soak my stupid heedless face because I said "okay."

It was about an hour before dusk and we would have had time, not lots of time, but more than enough, except that when we were halfway there, the light snow turned into a blizzard.

So there we were with snowmobiles in the middle of Lake Erie, a blizzard screaming around us. We could barely see with night beginning to fall. So we said fuck it, sat down and opened a beer, sharing the seat of Rocky's snowmobile to keep each other warm. It was really cold but still bearable, so one beer led to another as the night progressed. The snow died down and the sky began to darken, and the lights of the island appeared in the distance. We pointed them out to each other, laughed, clinked our bottles, and started up our engines, leaving our bottles in the snow, sitting beside each other, two friends watching the stars, and revved off. Rocky and I raced a mile or two, like the idiots we were.

He had the accelerator wide open when he hit the channel the icebreaker had left behind.

I don't think he had time to even notice. His Polaris 600 sank like a stone. It was gone before I even made it to the edge, but I grabbed his trailer as though it was the tail of a bull and held on while it tried to pull me into the black water after him. I'm leaning back and pulling, the futility of it all not having occurred to me yet, and both legs are in up to my knees before I let the trailer go, taking my left boot along with it. Then I hear a crack and the ice around my own snowmobile breaks open and it falls through. Like Rocky, it was gone in seconds, as though it had never been there.

I sat there for what must have been hours, confused about where I was and what to do, a merciful fugue having blunted the truth of what had happened. Eventually, the puzzle pieces left behind by the icebreaker refroze together. It took me a long time to walk home, my frozen left foot bleeding through my sock.

I wipe my face on a corner of my pillowcase, and my eye catches the side table that holds my second grade baseball trophy and my old catcher's mitt. Between them, there is a picture of the day Rocky and I ran away from home. His face is dirty, mine clean, his smile weak, mine broad. Over our shoulders are sticks, with kerchiefs containing our lunch tied to the ends. I pick up that picture, press it into my pocket, get up, and open the door.

ACKNOWLEDGEMENTS

A version of "Staying Put" was originally published in *Sabal: A Review Featuring The Best Writing of the Eckerd College Writers' Conference: Writers in Paradise*, July 2015: 56–67.

Thank you to the many friends and strangers who made this book possible.

Thank you to James Hand for telling me about ice conditions on Lake Erie.

In particular, I would like to thank the Crabapple Mews Collective – self-proclaimed "Crabbies" – but I can never see them as that. They have been joyful and generous midwives of this work. Never fainthearted, a particularly dauntless "Mewsie" carried my pages up a mountain during this collaboration. These are gifted writers and editors and I am very fortunate to have their careful hands on my work. My gratitude to them is boundless. And to Jane Cawthorne, whose own work is an inspiration to me: it's not just your prodigious talent or your comedic timing or your seemingly limitless ability to get things done. We gravitate toward you because you are that rare person who spreads joy in her wake. So glad to have been swept up in yours.

There are many other people who have helped me immeasurably in my literary endeavours and I very much appreciate the opportunity to thank them here. Many thanks to Hilary Flower for careful reading and ongoing encouragement. Thank you Tracy Lee Bird, good friend, gifted writer and editor extraordinaire. Thank you to David Pinto for your excellent notes and steadfast suspension of disbelief. Thank you to Dee Gill for judicious use of literary beer goggles. Thank you also to my willing and indispensable readers Lois Buxbaum and dear friend Donna Westbrook. Thank you to John Bruce for telling me I should. And thank you to Jackie Cappiello, for everything else. You are not Bubbie. Everyone is.

Tanya Coovadia has studied creative writing with such disparate literary talents as Michael Ondaatje, Denis Lehane, and Ann Hood. She completed her MFA in Creative Writing with the Solstice Program at Pine Manor College. Although born in Manhattan and now based in Florida, Tanya was raised in various small towns in Ontario, Canada, including Pelee Island where she spent many of her formative years.